GOLDEN HORSESHOES

An Illustrated Story By

Bill Smith

ISBN: 9798676683009

Golden Horseshoes is subject to copyright 2020 by Bill Smith and Advisor Resources, LLC, dba HI-ARTS. Original hardcover © 1990 by Bill Smith and Topwood Publishing. No part of this book may be reproduced or transmitted in any form or by any means, electronic or mechanical, including photocopying, recording, or by any information storage or retrieval system without written permission. Cover design, artwork and original book built by Bill Smith. This book is a work of fiction. Names, characters, businesses, places, events and locales are either the products of the author's imagination or used in a fictitious manner. Any resemblance to actual persons, living or dead is purely coincidental.

For book ordering, new book releases and updates, please visit:
HI-Arts.Art

GOLDEN HORSESHOES

Chapter 1

We had a freezing hard wind on our backs, that angry horse and I, as the sun brought first light to the massive mountain range east of Sacramento. As I led my horse up the ravine I turned back into the clear, cold wind they call Mariah and saw distant city lights twinkling in the early morning shadows.

My name is Woody, that's right, just Woody, and I call my horse Mariah after the wind. I'd made strong coffee, crisp bacon and biscuits in Gold Camp, saddled up, and have been up this trail at least an hour now. A week-long rain stopped yesterday, and I expect this ravine was a torrent of water just a while ago. We made a gentle right turn out of sight of the valley below and then an unexpected sharp left turn into a level area fifty feet wide and about as long.

At the far end of this rocky gulch where a ribbon water still fell over the ledge, Mariah and I eyed something we could not believe. He must have seen it the same time I did because we looked at each other in complete disbelief and then back to that gold. We walked up closer, real slow, like it might just disappear if we moved too fast. But there it was, a pocket of pure shining gold about four feet across and kind of oval shaped. It was like looking into one of those sawed in half geodes with all the even crystal shapes, only it was solid, pure, yellow gold.

After we had both overcome the kind of excitement that freezes you in your tracks, we sat right down to do some serious thinking. I hear gold can do unusual things to people, and those who find it had better be mighty careful how they handle it. We had to remember we were on the western slope of California's Sierra Nevada mountain range in the middle of the famous gold country where millions of dollars of gold and silver were mined in the 1850's, and most folks today don't recall the wild and strange things that happened to the people who first found the ore.

Not ten feet on either side of the gold was a tunnel dug by a miner sometime in the past. Yet here was a pocket of gold right under the surface that the miners had just barely missed.

Mariah was up and shoveling dirt with his hoofs about the time I had it all figured. First, we would pile rocks and dirt over the gold, and cover our tracks so that no one would find the gold. And we sure couldn't risk buying supplies in nearby Gold Camp without creating suspicion and starting a gold rush. No sir, it would take longer but we had to return to Sacramento. We had ourselves a plan, however, and what a plan it was.

Woody Spots the Pocket of Gold

Chapter 2

Mariah and I got off the mountain fast and pulled into town late afternoon the next day. Our first stop was at Mayfield Stables, which was a large old barn on California Street housing not only stables but also ample storage space and a blacksmith shop.

Here I purchased a used but sturdy buckboard with strong iron springs. Knowing full well that Mariah would never agree to pull anything on four wheels, I rented two healthy hauling horses from Mr. Mayfield and secured permission to store my wagon on his premises when not in use.

Our next stop was at the local undertaker, Mr. Walter Clopton Underhill, proprietor. I inquired of Mr. Underhill whether he might have a used, inexpensive coffin for rent. He replied emphatically that he did not, and that there was not, to his knowledge, a market for used coffins since most people preferred to use them permanently. I was obliged to purchase a brand-new model although I persuaded Mr. Underhill to provide a plain sandstone tombstone at no additional cost.

I have to admit at this point I was worn out. We had covered a lot of ground, but we still needed supplies before we turned in. I stabled the horses and headed for the B&P General Store. I could spend hours in this store examining the array of goods, smelling the fresh breads, and talking with friends, but what I wanted now was simple; a large steel cooking pot, a hand bellows, a can of brown paint with a brush, and a dozen flowers of any kind.

By the time the morning sun began painting burnt orange colors on the distant snow-covered peaks, we were at least two hours east of town and headed toward out mother lode of gold. Our hauling horses were pulling the buckboard at a healthy pace and as I turned to check on Mariah who was tied to the gate, I noticed high above the waking lights of the city a brilliant star in the west.

The next day, while a lantern shaped sun was setting beyond the Pacific Ocean, the horses, almost exhausted, pulled the wagon up Slide Canyon and right down the main street of Gold Camp. Without stopping to draw attention, I urged the horses up into the ravine. After we made the last two turns, one to the right and then left into the gulch, I untied the horses, gave them a good rubdown, and fed and tethered them for the night. They could sleep. I had a night's work ahead of me.

Chapter 3

The mine shaft just to the right of our gold was perfect for our purposes. A typical mining tunnel supported by old but heavy wooden beams, it ran at least thirty feet before a collapse had sealed it off. I unloaded everything from the wagon and brought the large steel pot and bellows a few feet into the tunnel. I gathered firewood until it was completely dark. Then the real work began.

I suspended the steel pot from a tripod, and underneath built a fire that had to be kept blazing hot most of the night. I then set about removing the rock and dirt that covered the gold.

Piece by piece, crystal by crystal, I loaded the gold into the steel pot for melting. Gold can be found in many rock formations, most of which are far more difficult to process, but this was a pocket of pure, beautifully shaped solid gold which would be simple for one man to manage. I continually fed wood to the fire and forced air into it with the bellows.

Each time a pot of the gold began to boil, I poured it into the flatbed of the buckboard and made a section a couple of inches thick. After ten pots of gold there were ten gold sections that together covered the bed of the buckboard. It looked to be about the size and shape of your front door only squared off into ten separate parts for easy handling.

While the golden buckboard was cooling and hardening, I started cleaning up. When I dug the gold out of the ground, I had discarded a blue mud. Miners in the 1850s had done the same, not knowing it was fine silver ore. I filled this and more back into the hole and smoothed it over. It appeared to me I had extracted all the gold in the pocket and was thankful it was just the right amount to fill the bed of my wagon.

Then I buried the steel pot and the bellows in the mine shaft and just before dawn when the gold had finally hardened, I took out the brown paint and painted the gold a nice buckboard brown. I then threw and kicked that coffin about 'till it looked like it was old and properly used. After throwing an appropriate amount of dust over the new wagon bed, I reverently placed the casket in the wagon, put the tombstone in the back covered with a Tarp, and gently set the flowers atop the casket. It was time to wake the horses. We were ready to move out.

Woody Pours the Buckboard Gold

Chapter 4

When the horses took their first pull at the new load, they stopped dead in their tracks, turned their heads and gave me the meanest longest stares horses can give. If looks could kill, I was six feet under. You see, Mariah had been with me a long while and he'd figured my plan already, but the only thing the other horses knew was that they had to haul this load all the way back to town.

I didn't expect any trouble on the road and I sure wasn't looking for any, but a man with a wagon load of gold has to be extra careful. We rolled slowly through Gold Camp looking casual and taking in the sights.

It took us until early evening just to get down the canyon, and the poor horses were beat. About the time we felt we were home free people-wise, it happened, and it happened fast. Three young buckaroos came riding around the bend with fire in their eyes. It was mighty obvious they were heading to Gold Camp to make some trouble, but they rode up on us first.

They surrounded us, all three grinning from ear to ear. The oldest, who was the biggest, said smugly, "Well, what do we have here?"

Now, I didn't greet them normal-like and I didn't act scared either. I kind of tilted my head to the side and twitched the side of my mouth real funny.

The fella to my left asked, "What's in the wagon, friend?"

I said in as high a voice as I could talk, "That's Grandpappy, killed in a gunfight over gold in 1890. We just dug him up. Takin' him back to the family plot to be with Grandma. You boys like to help?"

I was counting on the fact that even these wild buckaroos wouldn't be lifting flowers off an old coffin and snooping about. But this fellow on my left, he was pretty smart. He asked, "So, why's your wagon riding so low, friend?"

I said, "Darned if I know. Guess it's Grandpa's tombstone."

The younger rider was at the back of the wagon next to Mariah. The suspicious gent to my left ordered him to see what was under the tarp, and there it was, the sandstone tombstone looking heavy as can be. I kept my head tilted and kept twitchin' and looked back at Mariah. He'd gotten into the act too. He had his head sideways and his eyes crossed.

Well, all this was just too much for them. The young fella back by Mariah yelled, "Let's clear out. This guy's crazier that a barn owl and his horse is worse."

With that, they rode on into town, and all the way down the hill we could hear them hootin' and shootin' up Gold Camp just like it must have been in the old days.

I needed to melt this buckboard gold and turn it into negotiable pieces as quickly as possible. I intended to store the wagon and put up the horses back at the barn, and I planned to use the forge and the blacksmith's huge cauldron to melt down the gold.

Chapter 5

It is Sunday morning, the perfect time. Church bells are ringing, and the congregation is leaving the church for the big celebration parade. The gold is finally melted and bubbling hot in the giant black pot. While everyone is at the parade outside, I will be alone.

Now please understand, I wasn't trying to be devious or sneaky with this gold. In fact, I had good civic minded and charitable intentions for it. It's just that I thought if folks didn't know about it, then no problems would arise.

But sometimes a person can be completely bass-ackward wrong about things and this was one of those times.

I don't know whether it was a burr under his saddle or a note from the horn section parading past the barn, but that crazy horse of mine all of a sudden went berserk, bucking and kicking all over the barn. Mariah had just finished knocking everything off the walls when he crashed into me and smashed into the wagon. The tongue of the wagon fell across the pot of bubbling gold and it rolled slowly over on its side.

Covered in straw, dust and droppings, I sat on my backside dazed, watching the gold pour out of the pot and run in a winding little river across the floor, under the barn door and right out into the middle of the parade.

The band stopped abruptly and there was a terrible silence as Mariah crashed through the barn door into the parade and galloped into the little pool of liquid gold forming in the street. If you think you've seen a spooked horse before, you should see one with burning gold feet in the middle of a parade!

That horse, and I tell you I had developed a real affection for him, took off like the wind and ran whinnying down California Street clear out of town. I figured I'd never see or hear from him again.

So, there I sat with my mouth wide open, looking out the door with the whole town staring at me. Remember, I warned you that gold can do funny things to people, and horses too, it seems.

When the gold hardened, it took ten of us to stand it up on end. We all beheld the most beautiful, twisting and turning gold sculpture nugget the world has ever seen. It was between three and five inches around and measured fourteen feet ten inches long. It wandered and looped back and forth like a little twisting river all the way to the end. That was where the gold had stopped and formed a small pool about the size of a large frying pan. Of course, there were four perfectly round hoof sized holes in the center made by you know who.

Well, we may not have the largest gold nugget in the world, but I'll bet we have the longest, and I know for certain it's the most artistic. We needed a solution to a serious problem, however.

Where do you put a fourteen-foot ten-inch solid gold nugget?

The Parade Stares at Woody and Mariah

Chapter 6

The whole town, proud as could be, turned out to see the famous gold nugget installed in the bank. There was no way it would fit in the vault, so we fixed it securely on the wall about ten feet off the ground, horizontally, above and behind the teller's cage. It was in plain view for all to see and it wasn't long before folks all over the country heard about it and came to see it. The bank came to be one of the largest banks in the state because of all the attention and deposits the nugget brought in. I guess just seeing it there gave people a sense of security. Of course, after what I'd been through, I wasn't so sure I felt the same.

The bank was so appreciative, they made me a sizeable business loan, and three years later, for reasons I don't have the time or inclination to get into right now, I still haven't paid off that loan.

That is part of the reason a town meeting was called for tonight. Now, this requires some explainin', so here goes. You see, since I didn't have cash money to pay off my loan, the board of directors of the bank got together and decided they'd have to saw off about a foot of my nugget. This didn't set too well with me, but I had to be understanding of their problem. I mean, the bank had its own obligations and I had promised to pay them back. But it seems word got out about what the bank was fixin' to do and all heck broke loose. While I was willing to honor my promises, the entire town had other ideas. That nugget had become a symbol in the community, and a plan to saw into it was like cutting into civic pride.

An agenda for the meeting had been prepared but it immediately dissolved into the noisiest fracas you can imagine. After about two hours things calmed down and a settlement was negotiated. Since it was my gold, and since things were getting to the point where someone might get shot, I decided to speak in favor of the proposal.

It was agreed the bank could cut off ten inches of the nugget but it would have to be from the end called the 'doo drop' end, and not from the end which came to have many names, most popularly, the 'hot foot' end. This was because when the gold first ran onto the floor of the barn, it ran onto globs of you know what, which left a rather unattractive shape to it, if you understand my meaning.

Secondly, it seemed fair because the bank was taking a risk that the inside of that ten inches might be you know what. The final agreement relieved everyone, and all thought the proceedings were ended. The Mayor was just about to let the gavel fall when the town lawyer jumped up and insisted there was an issue yet to be resolved. "If Woody's nugget is to be sawed," he queried, "who is to have legal title to the gold sawdust, the city, Woody, or the bank?"

You can imagine the uproar. If it had been noisy before... Well, an hour later, order was restored. We all agreed that in the spirit of justice and fair play, and in order to benefit the entire community, the sawdust would be melted down and made into a much-needed front tooth for the Sheriff.

Chapter 7

Sheriff William "Doc" Rankin, to give you an impression, looks a lot like Buffalo Bill Cody. He is lean and handsome, wears a wide brimmed hat and has a handlebar mustache. But when he smiled you could see where he'd lost his front tooth in the defense of justice.

The Sheriff, we all call him Doc, wears two pearl handled silver six shooters and is such a good shot he'd never needed to shoot anybody...except once. He can throw three silver dollars into the air and keep them in the air 'till all twelve bullets are gone and his guns are back in their holsters. I've never seen him do it but there are enough folks in town who have, so I don't doubt it.

Winding up the town meeting, Sheriff Rankin was in the midst of an emotional Thank You for The Tooth speech when all of a sudden, he called for silence. Then we all heard it, a terrible screaming sound coming from down the street. Sheriff Rankin, as all good sheriffs will, was the first one at the bank with both guns drawn, hammers back and ready for action. As the rest of us caught up, he busted the doors wide open and there before us was a right funny sight.

You remember those three young buckaroos Mariah and I ran into a while back? Well, it seems they decided to rob the bank and make off with the nugget. And there they were. Two of them were on their backs, pinned to the floor by the nugget, squirmin' and hollerin', while the third one, you remember the smart fellow on the left, he was hopping around on one foot and holding the other in a whole lot of pain.

After much embarrassment and limited incarceration, all three of those fellows finally paid their dues and, interestingly enough, turned out all right.

Before I forget, I must tell you that the bank got its ten inches of gold and I was pleased to hear it didn't have a bit of you know what in it. Doc also got his gold tooth and would up wishing he hadn't.

Shortly after Doc's gold tooth was in place, an angry young gunslinger came to town and called Doc out. Doc would never back down, but he'd never shot anyone before, and he didn't want to break his record. But this young buck was persistent, and Doc found himself walking down the middle of California Street with the kid coming straight for him ready to draw. Doc never understood why some people get so all-fired pushy.

At about thirty paces Doc stopped cold, still staring the kid straight in the eyes. Doc was a formidable sight under any circumstances, but when the noonday sun glinted off his pearl handled silver Colts, you could tell the kid was having second thoughts. And when Doc slowly broke into that big, wide grin of his and the sun sparked off his solid gold tooth, the kid completely lost his composure and hightailed it out of town.

A couple of days later, however, while attempting to enforce the law, Doc got his tooth knocked out by a rowdy cowboy and in the scuffle the cowboy made off with Doc's gold tooth. When the cowboy stole Doc's tooth, he made his first mistake. Showing up in town again causing trouble and wearing Doc's tooth for all to see was his second, and last, mistake. They buried the gold sawdust tooth with the cowboy, and I hear tell the preacher had a slip of the tongue while reciting ashes to ashes, sawdust to dust.

The bank, on the other hand, sent its gold to the Carson City mint in Nevada to be turned into twenty-dollar gold coins. But after the gold coins were minted, the stagecoach was held up. Some of the gold was recovered, and two of the robbers were caught, tried and hanged. I've told you before this gold business can be mighty peculiar. For the present, we still had a situation on our hands that needed a solution. Where do you put a fourteen-foot gold nugget that cannot remain at a bank?

Chapter 8

The decision was unanimous. The nugget must go to the busiest place in town. The Golden Horseshoe Saloon had years ago become the general store and town meeting place. You could buy goods, post a letter, arrange transportation and drink a root beer, all under one roof. It was owned and operated by two ladies named Bee and Pea, which is why the establishment was once called the B&P General Store and Post Office.

The two gals are really quite sweet, and when they were naming the business neither wanted her name to go first so as not to offend the other. They solved that by painting a sign with a B on it and another with a P on it, and every January 24th they switched the order of the signs. They claim that day is when they opened their doors for business, and I don't doubt them. It's just that being as gold conscious as I have become, I can't help but remember that gold was discovered not far from here at Sutter's Mill in 1848, and you may have guessed, on January 24th. Next year it would have been called the P&B General Store and Post Office had it not been for their decision to change the name back to the Golden Horseshoe Saloon. This may seem confusing to you, especially since the Golden Horseshoe is not really a saloon at all, but the gals figured it would be good for business and, after all, they do serve root beer. But the main reason, of course, was that the big golden nugget with the horseshoe hoofprints was finding a new home.

The nugget was prominently displayed on the wall behind what used to be the bar, directly above a long mirror which was hung just above a long shelf. Centered on the shelf was a large plaster bust of President Abraham Lincoln. To the right of President Lincoln were neatly stacked cans of vegetables, and to the left was the community coffee grinder. Whether it was the change of name, the gold nugget, something else, or a combination of everything, no one knew for certain, but business began to boom. People were coming from miles around and were swapping stories about Mariah and me, and where we might have found the gold.

I heard one story repeated over and over about how folks had seen a horse with golden shoes flying cross the sky on nights when the wind was blowing full gale. As romantic as this sounds, I can tell you for a fact, that is just preposterous. I loved that horse and would be the first to exaggerate, but he would never even think about flying. Trust me. I knew him too well. Things went great for the gals and the town in general until one windy night we heard shouts mixed in with the church bells clanging. The Golden Horseshoe Saloon was on fire.

Chapter 9

The whole town joined in the bucket brigade but to no avail. The Golden Horseshoe Saloon went up like a bone-dry pine tree. In the early morning light, we pushed aside the ashes to see what remained of the goods and the gold. You remember where the nugget, the mirror and the shelf used to be. Well, on the ground just below, there were three gold cans of peas, a gold coffee grinder and, in the middle, a beautiful gold bust of President Lincoln.

There was no trace of the rest of the gold. It must have just bubbled away or done whatever gold does when it gets too hot. Needless to say, there was much sorrow at the passing of the world's longest and most beautiful gold nugget, as well as the Golden Horseshoe Saloon that really wasn't a saloon, and all its contents.

We had to melt the cans of peas, the coffee grinder, and, yes, finally President Lincoln. We hated to do it, but we needed every ounce of gold to rebuild and restock the Golden Horseshoe Saloon. It wasn't the first time President Lincoln had given his all for his country.

The President wasn't the only one to give his all because when everything was said and done, I was flat broke. I'd even lost my horse, which meant I was worse off than the day I'd first spotted that troublesome gold.

Well, that was many years ago, more than ten I expect. I headed out of town for a couple of days, and one thing led to another, and I haven't been back since. That's why Doc and I are up here now in the Yosemite high country at this beautiful lake, Tenaya it's called, after the Indian Chief. We met up last winter and decided it was time to return to town and take a look at all the changes.

We caught some rainbow trout today that we just cooked up with some butter and a big sweet onion. You folks that have done this kind of thing know there are few greater times in life. We stuffed ourselves with tasty trout and talked long and easy under the stars around our tall hot fire.

I was falling asleep when I heard a twig snap off in the pines, and then the rustling of brush. By the time my eyes were open, Doc was up on both knees with his guns out and ready. I heard that twig, but I never heard Doc who was right beside me. We stared into the darkness, straining to see. We heard a faint clopping sound, and into the firelight about fifteen feet off appeared the face of an old friend.

I hollered, "Mariah, you ol' horse! Where have you been all these years?" I mean, what else do you say to a horse you thought was gone for good? Then softly I said in the horse talk we always used, "Come on up to the fire and make yourself at home." I could tell he was a little uncomfortable, probably because he thought I was still upset about all the trouble he'd caused me. But my words seemed to comfort him some, and he slowly eased up to the fire. Between two tall pines, he raised up on his hind legs like he was trying to show us something, and that's when we saw them!

Shining low in the glow of the flames were four shoes of solid gold. They were worn down some, but there must have been a pound of pure gold on each hoof. I felt different emotions all at once. Mariah may have given me trouble, but I felt bad about what I'd gotten him into. I mean, he's been carrying all that weight on his hoofs all these years and had me to account for it.

It took Doc and me just a few minutes to get the golden shoes of all four hoofs. We placed them in front of the fire to watch them glow, and the three of us jumped for joy and danced a jig around the fire for I don't know how long. I'm not sure who was happier, Doc and I who were excited about seeing Mariah and the gold, or Mariah who was happy to be rid of it. After a while we settled down around the fire to catch up on old times, and we started talking about the gold and what it had done to us and a lot of other folks. To start with, it had only been a matter of hours since we first discovered the pocket of gold that it had gotten itself melted down into a buckboard and made Mariah and me act crazy in front of three kids, while carrying a coffin and a tombstone.

A Twig Snapped and Doc Was Ready

Then the gold got itself melted again, ran right out into a parade and had a horse run through it and carry part of it out of town.

A bit of it went into a man's mouth, then another's, and wound up buried back in the ground where it started.

Part of it was shipped to a mint, turned into coins, got two men hanged and ended up who knows where.

The biggest portion came to be admired on a bank's wall, finally dropped off and put three men in jail.

Then it went up onto another wall and turned itself into three cans of peas, a coffee grinder and a President of the United States...and the rest disappeared.

Doc looked at Mariah. Mariah looked at me. I looked at Doc, and then we did it in reverse. We were all thinking the same thing. We would have to be mighty careful with these four golden horseshoes or we'd just wind up in trouble again.

Well, everything turned out great for me, Doc and Mariah. Folks are still talking about the famous gold nugget, Doc's shining gold tooth, Mariah the flying horse, and soon, I'm sure, the golden horseshoes.

And you can believe that whenever I'm outdoors, I am always on the lookout. I figure since a horse with gold shoes walked up to my campfire once, maybe, just maybe, there's another one out there. So, if you should come across a horse with golden shoes, especially if she's a mare, please let me know because I have a horse she would love to meet.

Made in the USA
Middletown, DE
07 June 2022

66682185R00018